Balto of the Blue Dawn

NEW!

MAGIC TREE HOUSE® #54
A MERLIN MISSION

Balto of the Blue Dawn

by Mary Pope Osborne

illustrated by Sal Murdocca

A STEPPING STONE BOOK™

Random House 🏠 New York

Text copyright © 2016 by Mary Pope Osborne
Jacket art and interior illustrations copyright © 2016 by Sal Murdocca

All rights reserved. Published in the United States by Random House Children's Books, a division of Penguin Random House LLC, New York.

Random House and the colophon are registered trademarks and A Stepping Stone Book and the colophon are trademarks of Penguin Random House LLC. Magic Tree House is a registered trademark of Mary Pope Osborne; used under license.

Visit us on the Web!
SteppingStonesBooks.com
MagicTreeHouse.com

Educators and librarians, for a variety of teaching tools, visit us at
RHTeachersLibrarians.com

Library of Congress Cataloging-in-Publication Data is available upon request.

ISBN 978-0-553-51085-0 (trade) — ISBN 978-0-553-51086-7 (lib. bdg.) —
ISBN 978-0-553-51087-4 (ebook)

Printed in the United States of America

10 9 8 7 6 5 4 3 2 1
First Edition

This book has been officially leveled by using the F&P Text Level Gradient™
Leveling System.

For Bill Aquilar,
Mr. Bezo's best friend

CONTENTS

Prologue

One summer day in Frog Creek, Pennsylvania, a mysterious tree house appeared in the woods. It was filled with books. A boy named Jack and his sister, Annie, found the tree house and soon discovered that it was magic. They could go to any time and place in history just by pointing to a picture in one of the books. While they were gone, no time at all passed back in Frog Creek.

Jack and Annie eventually found out that the tree house belonged to Morgan le Fay, a magical librarian from the legendary realm of Camelot. They have since traveled on many adventures in the magic tree house and completed many missions for both Morgan le Fay and her friend Merlin the magician. Teddy and Kathleen, two young enchanters from Camelot, have sometimes helped Jack and Annie in both big and small ways.

Jack and Annie are about to find out what their next magic tree house mission will be!

CHAPTER ONE

Gold Dust, Stardust

Jack was reading on the front porch when Annie peeked out the door. "Bike ride later?" she asked.

"Sure," said Jack. "Let's go now, before it gets too dark. Tell Mom and Dad."

Annie slipped into the house to tell their parents. Jack closed his book about whales and sharks and stood up and stretched. He was tired from swimming at the lake all afternoon, but he felt good. He loved summer. A bike ride in the warm evening air seemed like the perfect way to end the day.

"Good to go," said Annie, coming out of the house with their bike helmets.

Jack and Annie ran down the porch steps and climbed on their bikes. They put on their helmets and pedaled out to the street. As they rode up their block, they waved to a neighbor mowing her lawn and to a couple walking two poodles.

"We need a dog!" Annie called back to Jack.

"What kind do you want?" he said.

"Any kind. I like all dogs," said Annie.

"Big or small?" said Jack.

"Well, both. I want a little dog and a big dog," she said. "And maybe an in-between dog, too."

Jack laughed. "Yeah, I'd like a dog," he said. "But probably just one."

"Whoa!" said Annie, putting on her brakes. "Did you see that?"

"What?" said Jack, stopping beside her.

"Above the woods—a bright flash of light," she said.

"You're kidding," he said.

"*Not* kidding! I had a feeling, even before we

left the house!" said Annie. Without another word, she bumped her bicycle over the sidewalk curb and headed into the Frog Creek woods.

Jack followed, his bike bouncing over roots and twigs in the shadows beneath the trees. Growing darker by the second, the woods were filled with the sounds of crickets.

"Am I brilliant or what?" cried Annie. She had stopped next to the tallest oak.

"Brilliant," said Jack, laughing.

The magic tree house was perched high in the oak. Their friend Teddy was grinning at them from the window. "It's about time!" he called. "I was getting ready to summon a crow or a rabbit to go get you."

Jack and Annie leaned their bikes against the tree and hurried up the rope ladder.

Inside the tree house, Teddy greeted them with hugs. "We must hurry," he said. "You are needed right away."

"Where? When? Why?" said Annie.

"Where? A seaside town in a vast territory

below the Arctic," said Teddy. "When? February 1925. And why? Because Merlin and Morgan believe you can save lives there."

"Whoa," said Jack.

"Sounds serious," said Annie.

"And cold," said Jack.

"It is quite serious, and it will be quite cold," said Teddy. "First, you'll need this." He handed Annie a small travel guide:

"Alaska? Oh, boy, I've always wanted to visit Alaska," she said.

"This guide was published in 1925," said Teddy.

"So it will be a different Alaska than Alaska today," said Jack.

"Precisely," said Teddy. "And you'll need this." He reached into his cloak and took out a small gold box. He handed it to Jack.

"What's this for?" said Jack. He started to take off the lid.

"No! Don't open it now," said Teddy. "There is a thimbleful of enchanted gold dust inside. It is from Morgan. You can use it only once."

"Use it for what?" asked Jack.

"In your time of need, you can use it to acquire a great skill that you both will share," said Teddy.

"Cool!" said Annie. "Like the time we used the magic mist of Avalon to give us the skill of great rock climbers."

"And the time we wished to be great magicians," said Jack. "And great horse trainers."

"And great soccer players," said Annie.

"Yes, a bit like all those times," said Teddy. "If you remember, on those missions, the magic lasted only for an hour. This time, the magic will last for *twelve* hours."

"Wow, that's a lot," said Annie.

"Yeah," said Jack, smiling. "That's a really long time to be great at something."

"But there is another difference," said Teddy. "Your skills on those past missions helped you solve your own problems. On *this* adventure, your great skill can only be used to save the lives of others."

"Hmm. So what kind of danger will others in Alaska be facing?" asked Jack.

"Merlin and Morgan didn't tell me that part," said Teddy. "I imagine they were quite sure you'd be able to figure it out when you arrived in the Alaskan Territory."

"We'll try," said Jack.

"One more thing," said Teddy. "Merlin wants those you help on this mission to be celebrated as heroes. He does not wish his magic to be part of their story."

8

"Okay, but how do we help without anyone knowing that we're helping?" said Annie.

Teddy reached into his cloak and brought out a second tiny box. This one was made of shimmering dark blue stone. He handed it to Annie.

She cradled the box in her hands. "It's so beautiful," she breathed.

"Do not open it until you need what's inside," said Teddy. "It holds a bit of stardust, very rare and very precious."

"Ohhh. What's it for?" whispered Annie.

"If you toss the stardust into the air and make a wish to be forgotten," said Teddy, "any memory or evidence of your visit will instantly be erased."

"Oh," said Jack. "Okay."

"Put the magic away now," said Teddy. "You must be on your way."

Jack hadn't brought his backpack, so he put the gold box in the pocket of his jeans. Annie did the same with the dark blue box.

"Ready," they said together.

Teddy reached into his cloak and
brought out a second tiny box.

"Be safe. Be well," said Teddy. "And do not freeze to death."

"Gee, thanks," Jack said. "Good advice."

Annie pointed at the cover of the travel guide. "I wish we could go to the Alaskan Territory!" she said.

The wind started to blow.

The tree house started to spin.

It spun faster and faster.

Then everything was still.

Absolutely still.

CHAPTER TWO

Quarantine

"Cold . . . face," Annie said, her teeth chattering.

"Y-yeah, yeah," said Jack. His breath billowed white into the sharp air.

"I feel like a fat b-brown bear," said Annie.

Jack laughed. He and Annie were covered with fur from head to toe. They wore fur pants, fur mittens, knee-high fur boots, and long fur jackets with fur hoods.

"Welcome to Alaska," said Jack. He pulled up his hood and tied it tightly under his chin. Annie did the same. Then they looked out the window together.

The tree house had landed in one of a few trees at the edge of a snowy field. Beyond the field was a coastal town. The winter sun was setting over an ice-covered sea.

"I wonder why we're needed to save lives here," said Jack.

"Do you think something scary is about to happen?" said Annie.

"Scary?" said Jack.

"Like an earthquake or a volcano?" said Annie.

"I don't know," Jack said. He picked up their guide to the Alaskan Territory. He pulled off one of his fur mittens, opened the book, and read:

About 12,000 years ago, people and their dogs crossed a land bridge over the Bering Sea from Russia into Alaska. When they reached Alaska, they became the first humans and dogs to live in North America.

"Cool," said Annie. "I like the dog part."

Jack kept reading:

> Until Russian explorers came to Alaska a
> few hundred years ago, only native Alas-
> kan people lived there. For thousands of
> years, the native people survived by mak-
> ing use of the few resources of the rugged,
> icebound land.

"Wow, they must be tough people," said Annie.
"No kidding," said Jack. He read more:

> In the late 1800s, the United States pur-
> chased Alaska from Russia, and it became
> a territory of the U.S.

"That's why this guide is called the Territory of
Alaska," said Jack. "It's from 1925—that's before
Alaska became a state."

"Got it," said Annie. "Okay. Let's go find some
lives to save."

"Wait," said Jack. "Where's our magic?"

"Check your pockets," said Annie. Annie pulled off her mittens, and they both reached into the big side pockets of their parkas.

"Got it!" said Jack as he pulled out the tiny gold box.

"Me too!" said Annie. She held up the tiny stone box.

"Gold dust, stardust," said Annie. "One to save lives, one to make everyone forget that we saved lives."

"Yep," said Jack. "Let's not lose them." They tucked the boxes back into their pockets and put their mittens on.

As Annie started down the tree house ladder, Jack crammed the Alaska guide into another one of his pockets. Then he clumsily followed Annie down the rope ladder in his bulky clothes.

As they started across the snow-covered field, their boots squeaked in the snow. Jack's throat hurt from breathing the dry, cold air.

In the fading winter light, they crossed a bridge

and walked along a frozen creek until they came to a boardwalk that ran along the icebound seashore. A sign said FRONT STREET. The town was empty. There were no old cars or wagons, only piles of ice and snow.

As Jack and Annie tramped through the snow, they passed stores and saloons and restaurants with crooked signs and broken windows. They all looked abandoned. There were only a few shops that looked as if they were closed but still might be in business: Nome Pharmacy, Nome Laundry, and Nome Bakery.

"I guess we're in Nome," said Annie.

"Good guess," said Jack. He took off one of his mittens, pulled out their Alaska guide, and found Nome. He read:

> Around 1900, gold was discovered in Nome, a remote Alaskan town on the Bering Sea. More than 30,000 gold seekers rushed to the boom town. But within ten years, Nome's gold rush was over, and the town fell on hard times.

The town was empty. There were no old cars or wagons, only piles of ice and snow.

"Hard times? No kidding," said Annie. "Nome looks more like a ghost town than a boom town."

"Let's keep going," said Jack. He pulled his mitten back on and put their guide in his pocket.

As he and Annie kept walking down the snow-covered boardwalk, they passed the Dream Movie Theater and the Golden Gate Hotel. Both had signs that said:

TEMPORARILY CLOSED.

Finally, they came to a white two-story wooden building that looked like someone's house. They could see lights and people inside. The black sign above the front door said:

MAYNARD-COLUMBUS HOSPITAL

"At least there are a few people in town," said Annie.

"But why is the hospital the only place that seems open?" said Jack.

"Yeah, weird," said Annie. They walked down the boardwalk until they came to a schoolhouse with a sign that said:

NO SCHOOL. QUARANTINE.

"Uh-oh," said Jack.

"Quarantine?" asked Annie.

"It means you're supposed to stay home so you won't spread a bad disease that's going around," said Jack.

"Maybe that's why everything is closed," said Annie. "I wonder what the disease is."

"I don't know," said Jack. "But if we go back to the hospital, we can ask someone there."

In the twilight, Jack and Annie hurried up the boardwalk to the entrance of the small hospital. When they stepped through the front door, they found a cold waiting room filled with people bundled in fur parkas and boots. Some seemed quite ill, slumped down in their chairs with their eyes closed. Others looked disappointed when they saw Jack and Annie, as if they were waiting for someone else.

Only one person stepped forward to greet them. A boy about fourteen or fifteen years old stared at them with dark, questioning eyes. "Who are you?" he asked.

"Our names are Jack and Annie," said Annie.

"Are you sick with diphtheria?" the boy said.

Annie shook her head. "No, we just arrived from the United States. Excuse me a second." She turned away from the boy and whispered to Jack, "What's diphtheria, exactly?"

"It's a dangerous disease from the past. That must be what the quarantine is for," Jack whispered. "We can't catch it. We had vaccines."

Annie turned back to the boy. "Do *you* have diphtheria?" she asked gently.

"No. My sister and my mother do," he said. "They are very sick in beds upstairs. I'm waiting for the special medicine to arrive. Dr. Welch says it will save their lives."

Before the boy could say more, Jack heard a man shouting in a room down the hall. "Hello! Hello! Can you hear me?"

The boy left the waiting room and hurried to an open doorway. Jack and Annie followed, and the three of them peeked into a doctor's office.

Two people were anxiously watching a man talk

on an old-fashioned black telephone. "Yes! This is Mayor Maynard in Nome!" the man shouted into the receiver. "Has the musher arrived with the medicine package yet?"

As Mayor Maynard listened to the person on the other end of the line, Annie whispered to Jack, "A musher is a person who drives a sled pulled by a team of dogs."

"I know," said Jack.

"That's a cool job," Annie whispered.

"No, listen to me!" Mayor Maynard yelled into the phone. "If Gunnar Kaasen arrives at the road-house in Solomon, keep him there! Do *not* let him and his team move on! We can't risk losing the medicine! We're expecting a huge blizzard tonight, sweeping down from the Arctic!"

A huge blizzard sweeping down from the Arctic? That's not good news, thought Jack.

"We cannot lose that medicine!" said the mayor. "Five have died already. There are at least twenty more cases. Possibly fifty. The Board of Health believes it is better to delay it than to risk losing it altogether! Tell Kaasen to wait until further word!"

"No! You can't delay it!" the boy said, barging into the office. "Gunnar Kaasen must keep going! The medicine has to get here soon!"

"I don't have a choice, Oki," said the mayor, hanging up the phone. "It's what the Board of Health has ordered."

The boy turned to a large rosy-cheeked woman. "Nurse Morgan, please don't let them delay!" he said. He sounded near tears.

"It's going to be all right, Oki," Nurse Morgan said, patting him on his shoulder. "Please go back to the waiting room."

"Don't worry," said a gray-haired man in a white coat. "I promise you, everyone is working night and day to fight this epidemic."

"Dr. Welch, my sister and mother need the medicine *now*, or they will die!" said Oki. "Even in a blizzard, I know Gunnar Kaasen can keep running!"

"You must leave us to do our work," said Dr.

Welch. He gently took the boy by the arm and led him back into the hall, where Jack and Annie were waiting. "Everything will be fine. Try to get some rest, son. We don't want you to get sick, too."

Then Dr. Welch stepped into the room with Mayor Maynard and Nurse Morgan and closed the door.

CHAPTER THREE

A Race Against Time

The Alaskan boy looked at Jack and Annie. "They can't delay!" he whispered frantically.

"It sounds like medicine is on the way," Jack said, trying to calm him. "It will arrive once the storm passes."

"But it needs to get here as soon as possible!" said Oki.

"The doctor said—" started Annie.

"The doctor can do nothing until the medicine arrives," Oki said. "But there is something *I* can do." He headed down the hall and hurried out the front door of the hospital into the dark. As he left, a gust of frigid air blew into the waiting room.

"That's it!" Annie said to Jack.

"What?" he said.

"Our mission! Help save the lives of these sick people!" Annie said. "That's why Merlin sent us here!"

"I think you're right," said Jack. "So let's talk to the doctor and nurse and find out what we can do."

"No, we should go," said Annie.

"Go where?" asked Jack.

"Go save Oki's life first!" Annie said.

"But he's not one of the people in danger," said Jack.

"He will be! He's going to do something crazy. I can feel it!" said Annie. "Come on!" She took off down the hallway and out the front door. Jack followed her into the icy cold. The moon was full and bright overhead.

"There!" said Annie. Before Jack could stop her, she took off after the Alaskan boy. "Oki, wait!" she shouted.

Jack hurried after Annie down the moonlit boardwalk. When they caught up with Oki, they were panting, their breath billowing into the air.

"Stop!" said Annie. "We want to help you!"

"How can you help me?" said the boy. He kept walking.

Annie and Jack fell into step beside him. "We came to Nome to help people fight the epidemic," said Annie.

"Only the medicine can help," said Oki. "They might *all* die soon if they do not get the medicine."

"Why can't they bring the medicine here by boat?" asked Jack.

"The sea is frozen!" said Oki. "Just look!"

"Well, what about a plane?" said Annie.

"No plane can fly at forty or fifty degrees below zero!" said Oki. "The pilot would freeze."

"Oh, yeah, you're right," said Jack. *Planes in 1925 must still have open cockpits*, he thought.

"A car?" asked Annie.

"No roads in winter," said Oki. "The only way

to Nome is by dogsled, over the mail trail."

"So what do *you* plan to do?" asked Jack.

"I will take a team of dogs and find Gunnar Kaasen," said Oki. "I will travel through the storm and bring the medicine back myself."

"But what about that blizzard?" asked Jack. "The one the mayor was talking about—the huge blizzard sweeping down from the Arctic?"

"Any good musher with a good team of dogs can handle a blizzard," said Oki.

"Where's your team?" asked Annie.

"My uncle Joe is a mail carrier," said Oki. "He has a team that runs to Port Safety and Solomon and beyond all the time."

"So your uncle Joe will go with you?" asked Annie.

"No. He has a broken leg from a sled accident," said Oki. "But I am not afraid to go alone."

Jack and Annie hurried alongside Oki, until they came to a shack on a spit of land near the frozen sea.

Jack and Annie hurried alongside Oki, until they came to a shack on a spit of land near the frozen sea.

In the bright moonlight, Jack could see that the shack was made of old driftwood and flattened tin cans. Smoke was rising out of a stovepipe on the roof.

"This is my uncle's house," said Oki. "And those are his huskies."

Next to the small house was a dog pen surrounded by a wire fence. A dogsled was inside the pen. Eight huskies were sleeping in the snow, their dark bodies curled up together to keep warm.

"Oh, wow," breathed Annie.

The dogs woke up at the sound of voices. They leapt to their feet and began yipping and whining.

"Hi, guys!" Annie said. She hurried to the fence to pet them.

"Careful!" said Oki. "They are very strong. They can jump up. . . ."

But Annie had an instant connection with the dogs. "You're so beautiful!" she said, reaching over the fence and rubbing different furry heads. "Hey, what's your name? What's *your* name?"

As Annie spoke, the dogs flattened their ears, and their lips curved into smiles.

"They really like her," Oki said to Jack. He sounded impressed.

"Yeah, Annie has a special way with animals," said Jack. "Especially dogs."

Oki smiled for the first time. "Do you and Annie want to come inside and get warm?" he said.

"Sure, thanks," said Jack.

Jack and Annie followed the Alaskan boy into the shack. Inside, a lantern lit a drafty room that smelled of fish and kerosene. Scratchy band music came from a wooden radio with big knobs.

"I must speak to my uncle. He is in bed," said Oki. He opened a door and slipped into another room.

Jack and Annie looked around. Strips of dried dark pink fish hung from a rack near the stove, which was made from an old metal barrel. Wooden barrels were set as chairs around a wooden table.

Voices came from the other room. Jack recognized Oki's. "But I *can* go alone!"

"No, you cannot!" said a deep, rasping voice.

Jack wondered if he and Annie should leave. It seemed wrong to overhear a family argument. "Let's go outside," he said to Annie.

"But we have to help fight the epidemic," she said.

"I know," said Jack. "Maybe it would be better to go back to the hospital and—"

"Listen!" Annie interrupted. She pointed to the radio.

The music had stopped. A news bulletin had come on: *"A desperate drama is unfolding in Alaska! In the town of Nome!"* the broadcaster said.

"Nome!" said Annie. She turned up the volume on the radio.

"All eyes are on this small icebound town in the northern territory, where an outbreak of diphtheria has already claimed five lives. Twenty of the best mushers and more than a hundred

and sixty dogs have been heroically running a relay across the frozen tundra. They must travel a total of six hundred miles to get medicine from Nenana, Alaska, to the town of Nome. . . ."

"That's us!" said Oki, hurrying back into the room.

"But now a blizzard threatens to curtail the efforts to save the residents of Nome," the announcer said. *"The storm is expected to sweep down from the Arctic, with forty-mile-per-hour winds and temperatures as low as thirty degrees below zero."*

"Oh, man," said Jack.

"It is unclear whether the mushers and their teams of heroic dogs will be able to continue," the announcer said. *"The medicine is now in the hands of champion musher Gunnar Kaasen. Will he and his lead dog, Balto, be forced to stop their lifesaving journey?"*

"Balto!" said Annie. "Didn't we see a statue of him in Central Park in New York?"

"Yeah, but I can't remember *why* he's so famous," said Jack.

"Me neither," said Annie.

"Will the blizzard keep the medicine from getting to the sick and dying in Nome?" the announcer said. *"It's a race against time! A race against death!"* Then the man's voice turned cheerful: *"And now we return to the music of King Oliver's Creole Jazz Band!"*

The lively music came back on, and Oki turned the radio off. "I'm going. I'm taking the dogs," he said. He grabbed a burlap sack hanging near the door and started filling it with dried fish. "I'll take this to feed them along the way. I'll find Kaasen. I know—"

"Do not go. Please."

Jack and Annie turned to see a native Alaskan man hobbling into the room on a crutch. He had long jet-black hair and wore a fur pullover with a hood. He had a weathered face and dark eyes. He barely glanced at Jack and Annie as he fixed his gaze on Oki. "If Gunnar Kaasen and Balto cannot travel in this weather, neither can you," he said.

"I can at least try, Uncle Joe," said Oki. "I have to." He kept throwing fish into the sack.

"Do not go out there alone, Oki," rasped his uncle. "You are not a champion like Seppala or Kaasen. And none of my dogs are as strong as Togo or Balto."

"It doesn't matter how great Kaasen is," said Oki, "if he is sitting at the roadhouse in Solomon."

"If he waits, he waits for good reason," said Oki's uncle. "Any team can be lost in a blizzard."

"Let me go, please," Oki said, facing his uncle.

"No!" shouted the man.

Jack held his breath as he looked back and forth from Oki to his uncle. Annie started to interrupt, but Jack shook his head at her. *This isn't our business,* he thought.

"I have run the trail many times," said Oki. "I can do it with my eyes closed."

"But I have always been with you," his uncle said. "You have never gone out alone."

"I have to try!" said Oki.

"Who will help you in a whiteout?" his uncle asked. "Who will help you if the ice breaks and moves out to sea? You will be gone forever."

"Maybe. But what about my mother?" Oki cried. "And my sister? They can't breathe! They can't swallow! They are on fire with fever! I promised them the medicine would arrive tonight. If it doesn't come soon, *they* will be gone forever. I have to hurry! You heard the radio! It's a race against death!"

Oki slung the sack of dried fish over his shoulder, picked up the kerosene lantern from the table, and hurried outside.

CHAPTER FOUR

Champion Mushers

"Stay with me, boy!" Uncle Joe called after Oki. But the man's voice was lost in the excited barking of the huskies in the yard.

"Excuse me, sir," Annie said. "What if *we* go with him?"

"Annie—" said Jack, shaking his head.

The man turned and looked at Annie and Jack as if noticing them for the first time. "Who are you?" he said.

"Jack and Annie," said Annie. "We're friends of Oki's, and—and—we're champion mushers."

"Stay with me, boy!" Uncle Joe called after Oki.

What? thought Jack.

Oki's uncle scowled. "Champion mushers? How can that be? You are very young."

"We *are* young," said Annie. "But we have great skills. Right, Jack?" She quickly added in a whisper, "Gold dust."

Oh, right, thought Jack. He nodded.

"We heard that lives were in danger here," said Annie. "So we came from the United States to help."

"Help how?" said Oki's uncle.

"Take a team of sled dogs and help get the medicine here," said Annie. "Right, Jack?"

Jack took a deep breath. He was a little nervous about losing their way and freezing to death, but he nodded again.

"We really want to help you," Annie said to Oki's uncle.

The man stared at them for a moment, his face lined with grief. "I don't know what to do," he said. "I lost my wife and my two children seven years ago in the flu epidemic. Nome lost more than a thousand people then. I fear it is about to happen again." Tears started down the man's craggy face.

Jack was stunned. *More than a thousand people died?*

"That *won't* happen again," Jack vowed. "We'll do everything we can."

"Thank you. But *please* leave my nephew here," said the man. "Do not let him go. Oki and his mother and sister are all I have."

"Don't worry. We won't let him go," said Jack.

"Take my team. They are good dogs," said Oki's uncle. "They have traveled the trail hundreds of times, delivering mail with me."

"We promise we'll take good care of them," said Annie.

"Thank you." The man bowed his head. "Thank you." Then he turned and hobbled with his crutch back into his room.

Annie took a deep breath. "This is a good plan," she said to Jack. "Right?"

"Right," he said. He hoped it was a good plan. He felt terrible for Oki and his uncle.

"Gold dust?" said Annie.

Jack took off his mitten, reached into his pocket, and pulled out the tiny gold box. He pried open the lid and stared at the glittering dust inside.

"It's so beautiful," breathed Annie.

Jack poured a bit of the gold dust into the palm of his bare hand. "We wish to be champion dog mushers to save lives," he whispered. Then he tossed the dust into the air. The room filled with a sparkling gold light. The light gathered around Jack and Annie, then quickly faded away.

Jack felt a rush of energy.

"Wow!" said Annie, grinning. "I'm ready to hit the trail. Are you?"

"Yep!" said Jack. "Sure am." He laughed.

"Quick, before Oki leaves with the dogs," said Annie. She started for the door.

"Wait," said Jack. "The magic works for twelve hours." He looked at a clock on the wall. It was eight-thirty. "We have to be back by eight-thirty tomorrow morning. No later."

"Got it!" said Annie. Then the two of them

hurried out of the shack into the freezing night.

The huskies were whining and leaping around the moonlit pen as Oki tried to buckle them into their harnesses. "Be still!" he commanded. "Be still!"

"Wait, Oki!" said Jack.

Wrestling with a dog, Oki looked up at Jack.

"Annie and I will look for Gunnar Kaasen!" said Jack. "Your uncle wants us to take the team by ourselves."

"By yourselves?" said Oki.

"Yes!" said Annie. "You have to stay here. He can't risk losing you."

"But how will you do this?" said Oki. "You don't know the dogs or the trail."

"We have great skills," said Jack. "And we trust the dogs. Your uncle told us they've traveled the trail hundreds of times."

"Yes . . . but—" said Oki.

"Good! Then *our* job is just to help them do *their* job," said Annie.

"And *your* job, Oki, is to stay with your uncle

and be near your sister and mother," said Jack.

"If you are out in the storm, your uncle will be sick with worry," said Annie. "And your mother and sister would not want that."

Oki stared out toward the frozen sea for a moment. He looked very troubled. "I want to go with you," he said finally. "But I will stay here for the sake of my uncle." He held the gate open so Jack and Annie could enter the dog pen.

"Come on, guys," Jack said to the huskies. "Let's buckle up!" He and Annie pulled off their mittens. Even in the dark, they had no trouble hitching the dogs into their harnesses.

"I'll get the rigging," said Oki. He grabbed a bundle of lines from the basket of the sled and began untangling them.

When Jack and Annie finished putting harnesses on all the dogs, they hooked the team to the rigging. They quickly and calmly attached tug lines to the harnesses and fastened neck lines to collars.

"Work with us, guys!" Annie said as they tried to hitch the excited dogs to the towline.

A lead dog jumped up and licked Jack's face.

Jack laughed. He knew not to scold the dogs and risk dampening their enthusiasm. The team would need their high spirits to run the tough race ahead.

Soon all the huskies were strung to the towline, lined up in pairs. The two lead dogs stood proudly in front, their tails high, their noses sniffing the air. The bells on their collars jingled.

Two swing dogs stood behind the leads. Two team dogs stood behind them, and two wheel dogs stood directly in front of the sled.

"You guys are the best!" said Jack.

The dogs whined and barked, as if eager to go.

"You are both very good with the dogs," said Oki.

"Be firm. Be fair. Give kindness and respect," said Annie. "That's how we always treat them. We promise."

"Thank you," said Oki.

Jack and Annie pulled on their mittens. "How far is Solomon?" Jack asked.

"About thirty-five miles," said Oki. "In about twenty miles you will pass the roadhouse in Port Safety. Maybe fifteen more, you will come to the roadhouse in Solomon, where you will find Gunnar Kaasen."

"Any idea how long the trip should take?" asked Annie.

"About five hours to get there," said Oki.

"So around ten to go and come back," Annie said to Jack.

"No problem. Where does the trail start?" Jack asked Oki.

"Just beyond the yard," said the boy, "where you see tracks in the snow."

"Got it," said Jack. He turned to Annie. "How about I drive first? You can sit in the basket, and then we'll switch?"

"Okey dokey," said Annie. The dogs were still

as she took her position in the basket of the sled. She sat on the wooden slats and held the side railings.

Jack stepped onto the long runners that extended behind the basket. He gripped the two handles of the sled, bent his knees, and leaned forward. He felt as if he'd driven a dogsled all his life.

"I'll get the snow hook," said Oki. He picked up a metal hook that anchored the sled to the snow. He put it in the basket in front of Annie. Then he added the sack of dried fish. "Dog food," he explained.

"Cool," said Annie.

"All set?" Jack asked.

"All set," Annie said. "Oki, please tell your uncle we'll take good care of his team."

"See you in the morning!" said Jack.

"Good luck!" said Oki.

"Line out!" Jack called to the dogs, knowing all the right commands to use. Bells jingling, the

lead dogs drew the team straight out in front of the pen.

"*Hike!*" Jack shouted. All eight huskies bounded forward and pulled the sled into the cold Alaskan night.

CHAPTER FIVE

Straight Ahead!

Moonlight cast a silvery glow over the icebound sea. The huskies' heavy breathing made a cloud over the team as it glided along the coast. The only other sounds in the darkness were the jingling bells of the lead dogs, the creaking of the sled basket, and the *swish* of the smooth wooden runners over the snow.

As the dogs did their job, Jack magically knew how to do his: He knew how to "pedal" the sled by pushing the ground with his right foot while keeping his left on the runner. He knew how to push in the perfect rhythm to keep the team from running too fast, so they wouldn't pant and hurt their lungs in the freezing air. He knew how to balance his weight and bend his legs to absorb the shock of bumps on the trail. He knew how to keep all the lines tight and straight, so none of the dogs would get tangled in them.

Jack knew all the musher commands, too. When the team came to a snowdrift, he shouted, *"Gee!"* to make the wheel dogs curve to the right.

When the team came to another drift, he shouted, *"Haw!"* to make the wheel dogs curve to the left.

When it was time to straighten out the towline again, Jack shouted, *"Straight ahead!"*

Every time the dogs did what Jack commanded, he said, *"Good dogs!"* But he hardly said more. He knew the fewer words, the better. The dogs depended on clear commands.

Riding in the sled basket, Annie was silent, too, though several times Jack heard her gasp and say, "Wow!"

"Wow!" is right, Jack thought. The windless Alaskan night was beautiful. Maybe the forecast was wrong. Maybe their ride would just be a thrilling race to save lives.

Mile after mile, the huskies ran along the well-worn trail. When the dogs raced down an incline, Jack dragged his heel to keep them from going too fast. When they labored up an incline, he lightened their load by hopping off and running beside the sled, holding on to one of the handles to keep it steady. When the trail was flat again, he jumped back on the runners.

"Good driving!" Annie called.

Jack smiled. He loved being a champion musher. He loved knowing exactly what to do and when to do it. But he especially loved the easy connection he felt with the huskies. Sometimes he even felt like a running dog himself as he pedaled in rhythm to their pace.

Lost in his thoughts, Jack failed to notice a change in the weather, until he heard Annie call out, "The storm's starting!"

*Mile after mile, the huskies ran
along the well-worn trail.*

Jack realized it had gotten colder and darker. Clouds covered the moon. The wind was blowing, and snow was falling. Snowflakes began to freeze on the lenses of Jack's glasses. Soon he couldn't see well enough to give commands to the dogs. Flying blindly down the trail, he tried to wipe his glasses with a fur mitten, but that only made it worse.

As the huskies headed into a sharp curve, Jack lost his balance. He slipped off the runners and tumbled into the snow. The huskies came to a halt and started barking.

"What happened?" Annie shouted.

"My glasses got messed up," Jack said, picking himself up. "I couldn't see anything."

"Don't worry, that happens," said Annie.

"I guess I was *too* sure of myself," said Jack.

"Even champion mushers have problems if they can't see," said Annie. "Let's switch places for a while. I'd love to drive."

"Sure, thanks!" said Jack. He climbed into the

basket and sat on the boards, while Annie took her position on the runners.

"Line out!" Annie commanded the dogs.

The team straightened out the lines.

"Good dogs!" Annie shouted. *"Hike! Straight ahead!"*

The huskies started running again. As they pulled the sled through the swirling snow, Jack took off a mitten and scraped his glasses with his bare fingers. When his skin started burning with pain from the cold and wind, he quickly put the mitten back on.

Annie kept a steady hand and a steady pace as she drove the eight huskies through the snowstorm. The wind blew harder, but she shifted her weight to keep the swaying sled from tipping over. She never let the towline go slack and get tangled with the other lines. Every time she yelled "Gee" or "Haw," Jack leaned to the right or left to help the sled around the curves.

When the dogs started up a slope, Jack knew he should lighten their load. "I'll get off!" he called to Annie.

"Easy!" Annie commanded the team.

As the huskies slowed down, Jack jumped out of the basket. "I'll run awhile!" he yelled.

"Okay, but stay close!" said Annie. Then she commanded the dogs to pick up speed again: *"Get up!"* The team easily dashed up the incline and sped along the frozen shore.

Jack decided to keep running. It felt good to move in the biting cold. Then suddenly he heard the grinding of the sled runners. The team was running over ice instead of snow! Jack heard a loud cracking sound beneath his boots. His feet had broken through the ice! His fur boots sank into a freezing puddle almost a foot deep.

The team sailed ahead of Jack, pulling Annie and the sled away from the ice. Left behind in the snowy dark, Jack tried to climb out of the crack, but more ice broke off. His feet were getting soaked!

"Annie!" he shouted. "Annie! Stop!"

"Gee!" Annie yelled. Jack could hear her turning the team around. He heard the bells of the lead dogs as they headed toward him.

"Whoa!" Annie brought the huskies to a stop.

"Stay back!" Jack shouted. "There's thin ice here! Keep the dogs back!" If the huskies got their feet wet, their soft pads would quickly stick to the ice and freeze.

Jack used all his strength to pull his boots out of the crack. He slipped and slid across the ice and snow as he made his way to the sled. "Come on, let's go!" he cried, climbing into the basket. "My feet are soaked!"

"Hike!" Annie yelled.

As the dogs took off through the bone-chilling cold, Jack felt his feet burning with pain. Soon they started to grow numb. As an expert musher, he knew that wet feet lost heat twenty-five times faster than dry feet. He had to get out of the cold immediately or he would suffer severe frostbite.

Before Jack could think of what to do, the

huskies slowed down and yelped with excitement.

"Oh, wow!" said Annie as the team came to a stop.

Jack's glasses were covered with ice again. "What is it?" he shouted, unable to see. "What's there?"

"We've come to a house!" yelled Annie. "There's smoke from a chimney! And there's a light shining inside!"

"Just in time!" said Jack. He climbed painfully out of the basket as Annie set the snow hook in the ground to hold the dogs. *"Stay!"* she commanded. She helped Jack through the blowing snow to the front door of a log cabin.

CHAPTER SIX

Port Safety

Annie banged on the wooden door.

A moment later, it opened. "Gunnar?" a man said, peering into the snowstorm.

"No!" Annie shouted. "The ice cracked and my brother fell through! His feet are soaking wet! Can you help us?"

"Hurry! Get inside!" the man said.

With Annie's help, Jack limped into the warm, firelit cabin. He took off his mittens and wiped snow and ice from his glasses.

"Sit near the stove!" the man commanded. "I'll heat some water!"

Annie helped Jack out of his parka, and he sat on a wooden chair near a crackling woodstove.

"Take off his boots!" the man said.

Annie helped Jack pull off his fur boots and wool socks, then set them near the stove. The man grabbed a kettle from the top of the woodstove and poured water into a bucket.

Jack looked at his wet feet. They were white and numb from the cold. He couldn't move his toes.

"How are they?" the man said, lugging the bucket to Jack.

"N-not bad," Jack said. He was still trembling from the cold.

"Not good," said the man, looking at Jack's feet. He set the bucket down in front of Jack. "Soak them awhile."

"Thanks," said Jack. As he put his feet into the warm water, he was overcome with pain. He started to pull them out, but the man stopped him.

"Keep 'em there, kid," he said.

"Okay," said Jack, gritting his teeth. Listening to the howling wind and the snow pelting the cabin windows, he worried about the huskies. "Can— can we bring our dog team inside?" he asked.

"Sure, I'll unhitch them from their harnesses. You stay here and soak your feet," the man said. Then he threw on a parka and hurried outside to get the dogs.

"I'll help him," Annie said to Jack. "Don't move." And she followed the man back into the storm.

As Jack sat alone in the one-room cabin and soaked his feet, he worried about the time. He looked around for a clock but didn't see one. How long would it take for his boots to dry? he wondered. Would his feet be okay? Did the dogs have frostbite, too?

Jack was glad when the door opened. "Everyone in!" Annie shouted. Hauling the sack of dried fish with her, she led the huskies inside.

The man followed the team into the cabin and slammed the door against the storm. "Go! Sit," he ordered the dogs. He pointed to dry straw spread over the floor. The bedraggled huskies took slow steps across the room and settled down in the straw.

"Feel any better?" the man asked Jack.

"Yes," said Jack. His teeth had stopped chattering, and the pain in his feet had lessened. "I'm Jack. She's my sister, Annie."

"I know, she told me," said the man. "I'm Ed." He grabbed the kettle and poured a little more steamy water into the bucket.

"Ed's a musher, too," said Annie. "His team is in a shed behind the cabin. He's a mailman, like Oki's uncle. He recognized their dogs."

"Cool," said Jack.

"Yep," said Ed. "Keep soaking your feet while your sister and I take care of the dogs."

Jack kept his feet in the bucket as Ed poured drinking water into a large pot and gave it to the team. Then Ed and Annie knelt in the straw and massaged the dogs' feet, one paw at a time. The huskies panted and looked as if they were smiling.

"Good dogs, good dogs," Annie kept saying.

"That's right, good dogs," Ed chimed in.

Jack saw that the musher was missing teeth and his beard was scraggly. Even so, his face had dignity and strength, Jack thought. Now that he understood the job of a professional musher, he admired Ed a lot.

"Ed lives here, at the Port Safety roadhouse," Annie said. "That's a good name for it, huh?"

Jack nodded. As the wind howled outside, it *did* feel safe inside the cabin, but he worried that they couldn't stay. They had only twelve hours of magic. "Do you know what time it is?" he asked.

"Hold on." Ed pulled out a pocket watch. "Almost midnight," he said.

So almost eight and a half hours left to find Gunnar Kaasen and return to Nome, thought Jack. Suddenly he remembered something. "Ed, why did you call us Gunnar when you opened the door?"

"Did you mean Gunnar Kaasen?" asked Annie. "Were you expecting him?"

Jack kept his feet in the bucket as Ed
poured drinking water into a large pot.

"I *did* mean Gunnar Kaasen," said Ed. "Earlier today I was told to wait for him. If he gets tired on his journey, I'm supposed to take his package on to Nome. But then I got word from Solomon that Gunnar would be staying there awhile. When I heard a knock, I thought he'd decided to push on."

"No," said Annie. "The mayor of Nome told him to wait until the storm ends. At least that's what someone told us."

"Good thing," said Ed. "Only a crazy fool would drive in a storm like this. So why the heck were you two out there?"

"Uh . . . well, we just went out for a short ride to . . . uh . . . ," said Annie.

"To exercise Oki's uncle's dogs," said Jack, "while Oki's at the hospital."

"Right," said Annie. "And then we got lost."

"You're lucky you found this place before you froze to death," said Ed.

"Yeah. Really lucky," said Jack.

"How are your feet?" Ed asked him.

Jack pulled his feet out of the water. His skin was pink, and the terrible pain was gone. He wiggled his toes. "I think they're going to be okay," he said.

"Good news," said Ed. He grabbed a towel and a pair of socks from an old canvas bag and tossed them to Jack. "These socks will be too big, but better big socks than wet ones."

"Thanks," said Jack, drying his feet, then pulling on the warm, woolly socks.

"You just dodged a case of frostbite, mister," said Ed. "I bet you kids will think twice before taking a joyride in a blizzard again."

"Well, actually, I think we should be heading home soon," said Jack. "But don't worry. It's not far."

"*What?* Are you two crazy? In this weather?" said Ed.

"Well, we're, um, champion mushers," Annie said in a small voice.

"Oh, yeah?" Ed squinted at her. "What races have you won?"

"Well . . . um . . . they weren't in Alaska," Annie said. "We, uh . . . we won the Frog Creek Winter Relay and—"

"Never heard of it," said Ed. "Doesn't matter. I don't care who you are; you're not going back out in that storm. Your team needs to rest, if nothing else. And eat! Right, fellas?"

Ed grabbed the burlap sack and pulled out flat pieces of dried pink fish. The huskies wiggled and whined as Ed started feeding them.

Annie looked at Jack. "Maybe we can stay a little bit longer?" she said under her breath.

Jack nodded. "Okay. But we have to keep our eye on the time."

"We will," said Annie.

The dogs gobbled up every piece of fish and drank from bowls of water. Then the huskies sat down, put back their heads, and began to howl. The wind howled outside as all eight dogs howled inside.

Jack knew the howling meant the dogs were satisfied. He, Annie, and Ed laughed, until the howling stopped as abruptly as it had begun.

The dogs then began nodding happily off to sleep, one by one. Some lay on their sides, while others curled up in tight balls and covered their noses with their bushy tails.

"All right! Now let's get *you* some food and drink!" said Ed.

"Can you please tell us what time it is again?" asked Jack.

Ed glanced at his watch. "One-fifteen," he said.

Jack didn't know what to do. He was hungry, but now they only had seven hours left to find Gunnar and get back to Nome.

"I'll make some soup," said Ed. He seemed determined to keep them from going back out into the blizzard. He grabbed a can of tomato soup from a shelf and began opening it with a can opener.

What about our mission? Jack wondered. How could he make Ed understand that they had to leave? "Excuse me," he said. "I'm afraid—"

"You can wash your hands over there!" Ed

interrupted. He pointed toward a tin basin on a washstand.

"It's okay," Annie whispered to Jack. "We have time." She put her red chapped hands into the cool water and washed them with soap. Jack reluctantly did the same.

Ed nodded toward the table. "Sit!" he said, as if giving a command to two huskies.

Jack and Annie smiled. They dried their hands and sat on two wooden barrels at the table. Ed dropped a box of soda crackers between them and gave them each a glass of milk. While the blizzard raged outside, he filled two bowls with steamy soup from a pot on the stove and put them in front of Jack and Annie. Then he sat in an old armchair near the table.

"Thanks, Ed!" said Annie.

"Yeah, thanks," said Jack, sighing. Breathing in the delicious smell of the tomato soup, his worries momentarily faded.

CHAPTER SEVEN

Jingle Bells

"Mmm, delicious!" said Annie. She and Jack slurped down the hot soup. As they chewed the salty soda crackers, they watched the dogs breathe peacefully in their sleep.

"Do most Alaskans have sled dogs?" asked Annie.

"Many do," said Ed, resting in his armchair near the fire. "But the day is coming when dogs won't be used much anymore, except for racing. I can see it happening already. Small planes will get better and better and take over the long trips.

Cars will improve, and roads, too. Soon enough, we'll have vehicles that go through deep snow in no time."

"That's good in a way," said Jack. "It'll help medicine travel faster."

"But it's sad, too," said Annie.

"I'm with you, missy," said Ed, looking at the sleeping dogs. "Breaks the heart of an old-timer like me. People have used sled dogs for hundreds of years in this territory. I myself have known many brave dogs during my lifetime."

"Do you know Balto?" said Jack. "Gunnar Kaasen's dog? We've heard of him."

"Sure do," said Ed. "Balto is the best lead dog in Alaska, along with Togo, Leonhard Seppala's dog. Both Togo and Balto have stopped here on runs with Seppala and Kaasen."

"What's Balto like?" asked Annie.

"Ahh, that dog loves to run a trail," said Ed. "Loves it more than any dog I ever saw. Great strength and lots of courage. Big shaggy black dog. Beautiful to watch because of his spirit."

Annie smiled. "I'd like to meet him."

"Annie has a special way with dogs," Jack explained.

"With *all* animals, really," said Annie.

Ed smiled at her. "Alaskans are real respectful of animals, too," he said. "We wouldn't have survived a minute without 'em. People here have learned to use all the gifts this frozen world can give."

"Like what?" asked Jack.

"Well, the socks I just gave you are made of sheep's wool," said Ed. "The parkas that are drying over there are made of squirrel fur. We all wear sealskin pants and reindeer boots and fox fur hats. I wear moose skin and caribou skin and rabbit fur. The medicine headed for Nome is wrapped in bear hide. The medicine itself is made from horse serum."

"What's serum?" said Jack.

"The blood of a horse," said Ed. "It has antitoxins to kill diphtheria."

"Wow," said Annie. "So Alaskans get gifts

from"—she held up one finger after another—
"sheep, squirrels, seals, reindeer, foxes, moose,
caribou, rabbits, bears, horses . . ."

"And dogs," said Jack, finishing his milk.

"And dogs, of course," said Annie.

"And fish and whales and birds of the air. *All*
creatures," said Ed.

"So everything's connected," said Annie.

"That's right," said Ed, nodding. "Eventually it
all becomes one thing . . . the people, the land, the
animals, the sea, and the air—it becomes Alaska."

"Cool," said Jack.

The three of them stared for a long moment at
the dogs. Some of the huskies paddled the air with
their paws, as if they were dreaming about running over the trail.

Ed yawned, and his eyes started to close. A
moment later, his head drooped forward, and he
was snoring.

Jack quietly put down his spoon. He tiptoed to
the stove and grabbed his fur boots. They were dry,
but his socks were still damp. So he pulled the boots

over the big pair of socks Ed had given him. "It's time to head to Solomon," he whispered to Annie. "We have to finish what we came here to do."

Annie nodded.

Ed snored loudly as Jack and Annie silently pulled on their fur parkas. They grabbed their mittens and slipped over to the dogs and gently woke them. The dogs jumped to their feet. Even though there were whines and yips, Ed kept snoring.

"Thanks, Ed," Jack whispered to the sleeping man.

"Yeah, thanks for being so nice to us and the dogs," whispered Annie. Then, very quietly, she led the team out of the log cabin. Jack followed, closing the door behind them.

Outside, the wind and snow were blowing wildly. Jack and Annie pulled off their mittens long enough to harness the team. They nimbly hooked the dogs to tug lines, neck lines, and the towline.

"Ready?" Jack shouted above the wind.

"I hope Ed doesn't worry about us when he wakes up!" Annie shouted back.

Jack and Annie pulled off their mittens long enough to harness the team.

"Oh, man. I just thought of something," said Jack.

"What?"

"Stardust!" said Jack. "For Ed!"

"Yes!" said Annie. Leaving the dogs waiting for a moment, she and Jack hurried back to the cabin, slipped inside, and closed the door.

Ed was still snoring.

Annie reached into her pocket and took out the dark blue box. When she opened the lid, the silvery dust shimmered like starlight. She emptied a small amount into her palm and tossed the glittering dust into the air, whispering, "We wish to be forgotten!"

The stardust flashed through the room, then quickly evaporated. To Jack's amazement, the bowls, spoons, and cups were clean and stacked neatly on the counter. Jack's damp socks had vanished. The unopened soup can was back on the shelf. The hay was neatly spread across the floor.

"No sign we were here," said Annie.

"Except Ed will be missing a pair of his socks," whispered Jack.

Annie laughed. "Full speed ahead!" she whispered. Then she and Jack slipped back outside into the storm. They ran through the blowing snow to their waiting team.

"I'm happy to drive for a while!" Jack shouted in the wind. "Is that okay with you?"

"Sure! I'll take over whenever you want!" said Annie. She picked up the snow hook and put it into the basket, then climbed in herself.

Jack stood on the sled runners, crouching slightly and gripping the handlebars. "Okay, team! Ready to find Gunnar and save lives?" he said.

The huskies barked, as if saying *YES! YES! YES!*

"Ready, willing, and eager!" said Annie.

"Line out!" Jack commanded.

The team pulled the towline straight out, making it taut.

"Hike!" said Jack.

The eight huskies surged forward. Bells jingling, the team raced away from the roadhouse of Port Safety, pulling the sled through the blizzard.

As the basket bounced and bumped over un-even ridges on the trail, Annie almost fell out, but she didn't complain. Jack could hear her laughing, as if she were enjoying the ride.

The wind from the frozen sea was bitterly cold. As the wind howled and snow whirled through the dark, the dogs kept their heads down and ran on and on.

Jack used his skills to move the team around banks of drifting snow. Through gale-force winds, he drove the sled over the rough, frozen path at the edge of the sea.

Like sand in a sandstorm, ice crystals beat against his face, stinging his skin. His mittens were nearly frozen to the wooden handles. But he felt protected in his thick fur clothing. He was grate-ful to all the creatures that had given their gifts to help Alaskans survive in their frozen world.

As more and more snow stuck to the lenses of his glasses and turned to ice, Jack knew he shouldn't keep driving. "We need to switch now!" he called to Annie.

Before he could give a command to stop the dogs, a fierce gust of wind slammed against the sled, sending it into a bank. Jack fell off the runners and was swallowed up in a pile of snow.

"Jack!" cried Annie. "Where are you?"

"Here! Here!" said Jack, floundering as he tried to get up. His heavy fur clothing made it hard for him to stand, but Annie grabbed his hands and helped him to his feet.

Together they pulled the sled out from the snowbank and untangled the rigging.

"I can drive for a while!" said Annie.

"Okay!" said Jack. He sat in the basket.

Annie stood on the runners. *"Line out!"* she shouted.

The dogs straightened their lines. But before Annie commanded them to take off, she yelled, "Jack! Listen!"

Jack listened. He heard the shriek of the wind and the whooshing of snow. "Listen to *what*?" he said.

"Bells! I hear bells!" Annie shouted. "Up ahead!"

Now Jack could hear the bells, too—jingling bells. "Yes!" he said. "Another dog team must be coming toward us!"

"Could it be Gunnar Kaasen and Balto?" shouted Annie.

"Maybe!" yelled Jack.

The jingling bells grew closer . . . and closer!

"Yay! They're coming this way for sure!" shouted Annie.

But the sound of the bells stopped suddenly. Then through the storm came the frantic, high-pitched barking of dogs.

CHAPTER EIGHT

Catastrophe

Uncle Joe's team of huskies answered with yowling and yelping.

"Something's wrong!" cried Annie.

"Maybe they had an accident!" said Jack. "Let's check it out!"

"Hike!" yelled Annie. *"Straight ahead!"*

The team took off.

Annie drove the huskies through the dark toward the frantic barking. Soon they came to another team of dogs floundering in a snowdrift.

A sled had crashed and flipped over. The driver was trying to free his dogs.

"Whoa!" Annie ordered. *"Stay!"* Jack planted the snow hook firmly in the ground to secure their team. Then he and Annie bowed their heads against the wind and trudged through the gale.

"Gunnar?" shouted Jack. "Gunnar Kaasen?"

The driver waved and shouted, "Yes!"

"Oh, wow! We were sent to help you!" cried Annie. "Are you okay?"

"Yes! Just hit a bump back there!" said the famous dog musher. "The sled went flying and crashed on its side!"

Annie and Jack began helping Gunnar. They grabbed each dog by its harness and, one by one, pulled them out of the soft snow. By the time the dogs were all on their feet again, Jack had counted thirteen huskies.

Jack and Annie helped Gunnar turn the sled upright, setting it back on its runners. Then together, all three stomped on the snow with their boots, packing it down so the dogs could pull the sled out.

"Line out!" Gunnar commanded his team.

Soon the dogs were lined up in pairs in front of the sled, with a single dog in the lead.

"Wait, is that Balto?" shouted Annie.

"Yes!" said Gunnar.

Annie hurried to the front of the line. "Hi, Balto!"

Balto barked a greeting and leapt up to lick Annie's face. The bells on his collar jingled wildly. She laughed and hugged him. "I've wanted to meet you for a long time!" she shouted.

"Do you have the medicine for Nome?" Jack asked Gunnar.

"Yes!" the musher said, leaning over the sled. "It's right here—Oh! No! *No!*"

"No what?" said Jack. "What's wrong?"

"The package is missing!" Gunnar yelled.

"Missing?" said Jack.

"Where is it?" cried Gunnar. "Where is it?"

"Where is it?" Jack echoed.

"It was tied to the sled!" shouted Gunnar. "This is a catastrophe!" In the biting wind, the musher fell to his knees and frantically dug through the snow, looking for the medicine package.

"What's wrong?" Annie called from the front of the line of dogs.

Jack ran to her. "He lost the medicine! It fell off his sled!" he said. "We have to help him find it!"

"Wait, wait!" said Annie. "I'll bet *Balto* can find it!" She crouched beside the lead dog and unhooked his tug line and neck line.

"No, don't unhook him!" said Jack. "We can't lose Balto, too!"

"We won't lose him!" said Annie. "He can help."

She grabbed the lead dog's head between her mittens and put her face close to his, saying words Jack couldn't hear. Then she released Balto. "Find the medicine! Find it now!" Annie yelled.

While Gunnar crawled around in the snow looking for the package, Balto took off in the direction his team had come. With his nose to the ground, the husky trotted back down the trail.

"Let's follow him, Jack!" cried Annie. Leaving Gunnar and the rest of the dogs behind, she and Jack hurried after Balto. They trudged through the snowstorm after the eager dog, following the jingling of his collar bells.

When Annie and Jack reached Balto, he was whining and digging through the snow.

"I think he found it!" Annie shouted.

Jack felt around in the windswept snow until he touched something soft and solid. He pulled a heavy, fur-wrapped bag out of the snow and struggled to stand up with it.

"Great job, Balto! You found it!" shouted Annie.

"Gunnar!" Jack yelled. "We found the package!" But his voice didn't carry through the storm. "Let's take it to him!" he said to Annie.

Balto started back the way they'd come, his collar bells jingling. Carrying the package of life-saving medicine, Jack followed Balto and Annie.

When Annie and Jack reached Balto,
he was whining and digging through the snow.

When they reached Gunnar's team, Annie quickly hooked Balto to the front of the line. Then she and Jack hurried to Gunnar. The musher was still on his knees, not far from the sled, wildly shoveling through the snow with his hands.

"Gunnar, it's okay!" shouted Jack. "We have the package! It was back there! It must've fallen out when you hit the bump."

"Balto found it!" said Annie.

Gunnar gave a happy shout and staggered to his feet. Jack handed over the fur-wrapped package, and Gunnar tied it tightly to his sled.

"You go ahead, we'll follow you!" Jack shouted.

"We can help you if you need us again!" said Annie.

"Thank you!" shouted Gunnar Kaasen. "I won't forget you! Thank you!"

Annie yelled good-bye to Balto. Then she and Jack hurried back through the whirling snow to their own sled. The huskies greeted them noisily.

"Ready, team!" Jack yelled, pulling up the snow hook. "You're going to follow Balto!"

"Can I drive?" Annie shouted.

"Sure! We can switch places at Port Safety, if you want!" said Jack.

As he climbed into the basket, Jack thought about the Port Safety roadhouse. He wondered if Gunnar planned to stop there. It would be weird to meet Ed all over again, as if for the first time.

Annie stood on the runners and waited. Soon jingling bells could be heard. Moments later, Gunnar's team dashed by. With Balto in the lead, all thirteen huskies pulled the musher and his sled over the snow.

As the jingling faded into the night, Annie shouted, *"Hike!"* The eight huskies bolted forward and got back on the trail, dashing after Balto's team.

As Jack bumped around in the basket, he held on to the sides and closed his eyes against the fury of the storm. It wasn't long, though, before he heard Annie shout, "Port Safety roadhouse up ahead!"

Jack opened his eyes and saw the log cabin.

"Jack, look! Gunnar kept going!" yelled Annie. "He didn't stop at the roadhouse!"

"Keep following them!" said Jack.

"*Gee!*" Annie yelled, and swung her dogs away from the roadhouse.

Jack and Annie's huskies kept following the jingling bells of Balto as he and his team led the way north to Nome. Racing along the coast of the Bering Sea, Jack and Annie's team seemed even livelier and stronger than before. It was as if Balto was leading their team as well as his own.

Guided by Balto's spirit, all twenty-one dogs flew over the flat shoreline. As they ran, the weather improved. The snow stopped falling, and the wind died down. Amazingly, in less than three hours, the blizzard had stopped completely. The sky had begun to clear.

In the early gray dawn, Jack saw a church steeple in the distance. He saw lights flickering in the windows of houses.

"We're back! We made it to Nome!" he cried.

"Hurray!" said Annie.

The sun was rising as they followed Balto's team into town.

"We should take these guys back to Oki and Uncle Joe!" said Annie.

"You're right!" said Jack. "Gunnar's good now! The medicine's arrived!"

"Haw!" commanded Annie. And the dogs veered left and headed for the spit of land near the frozen sea.

In the early light, the huskies stopped at Uncle Joe's shack. As the dogs whined and yelped, Oki flew out the front door. His uncle followed, hobbling on his crutch.

Though exhausted, the dogs had enough energy to jump up and down and bark excitedly as their two friends greeted them with great joy.

CHAPTER NINE

Balto of the Blue Dawn

Jack climbed out of the sled as Annie stepped off the runners. A thin layer of ice covered their faces and clothes, but they were both laughing as they stamped their feet and swung their arms.

"You made it back!" Oki shouted.

"What time is it?" asked Jack.

"Almost six o'clock!" said Oki.

Jack smiled at Annie. "With time to spare!" he said.

"Thank God you are safe!" said Uncle Joe.

"Did you find Gunnar Kaasen?" Oki asked.

"We did!" said Annie. "On the trail below Port Safety! His sled had overturned. The medicine was lost, but Balto helped us find it!"

"Gunnar and his team arrived in Nome just ahead of us," said Jack. "They're delivering the medicine to the hospital!"

Uncle Joe closed his eyes and sighed with relief. Oki couldn't stop grinning. He pumped Jack's mittened hand, and Annie's, too. "Thank you! Thank you! You *are* champions!"

"Don't thank us!" said Jack. "Thank your dogs—they're the real champions!"

Oki opened the gate to the dog pen. The team of huskies walked in, panting wearily. Jack and Annie helped Oki and Uncle Joe unhitch the dogs from their neck lines and tug lines and pull off their harnesses. Then they massaged the dogs' backs and legs.

Oki gave the dogs water, and Jack and Annie fed them dried fish. The huskies wolfed down their meal and then howled with gratitude. As the sun rose over Nome, the eight brave dogs curled their bodies into the bright snow, covered their noses with their tails, and closed their eyes.

"Take a long rest, team," said Jack.

"You deserve it," said Annie.

"Let's go to the hospital," said Uncle Joe.

"Yes!" said Oki.

"We'll walk with you," said Annie.

Uncle Joe hobbled on his crutch as the four of them headed to town. Reflecting the brilliant blue of the early-morning sky, the snow itself looked blue.

By the time they arrived at the hospital, a small crowd had gathered. Jack saw Mayor Maynard and Gunnar Kaasen surrounded by a group of reporters with cameras and notebooks.

Gunnar's huskies were off to the side. Children were petting them, and photographers were taking pictures. As the dogs smiled and panted, Jack could see their clouds of white breath.

"The newspapers are here!" said Oki. "The whole world will soon hear this story! We will tell everyone what you have done, Jack and Annie.

They will honor you, too!"

Oki and his uncle walked faster.

"Whoa, wait," Jack said to Annie. "Stardust."

"Right." Annie reached into her pocket and pulled out the dark blue box.

"Are you coming?" Oki called back to them.

"Yes! We'll be right there!" shouted Jack.

As Oki and his uncle headed toward the crowd, Annie lifted the lid of the tiny box. Silvery powder shimmered inside. "We wish to be forgotten by everyone who saw us on our mission!" Annie said. Then she tossed the contents of the box into the air.

Like tiny grains of windswept snow, the stardust flashed brilliantly over the street. Before anyone could even look up, the silver dust evaporated, and the sharp, crisp air was clear again.

Annie put the tiny box back in her pocket. "Done," she said.

Then she and Jack headed toward the gathering in front of the hospital. When they drew close to the crowd, Oki caught sight of them—but then he looked away, as if he'd never seen them before. His uncle did the same. Gunnar Kaasen also glanced in their direction, but his eyes passed over them without interest.

"I guess it worked," said Jack.

"Yeah, no one remembers us at all," Annie said. She sounded sad. Jack felt a little sad, too.

"Mayor Maynard! Tell us about the heroes of the great serum race!" a reporter said.

Mayor Maynard proudly stepped forward. "For five and a half days, twenty mushers and more than a hundred and sixty dogs hauled the lifesaving medicine to Nome!" he proclaimed.

"How many miles was that?" a reporter asked as he scribbled on a pad.

"Nearly seven hundred miles!" said the mayor. "And two of our citizens from Nome heroically took part in the relay—Leonhard Seppala and Gunnar Kaasen. Both mushers had strong lead dogs. Leonhard and his dog Togo ran across frozen Norton Sound to Golovin, and Gunnar and his dog Balto brought the medicine from Bluff to Nome!"

Another reporter yelled to Gunnar Kaasen, "Congratulations, Mr. Kaasen! To what do you owe the success of your part of the relay?"

"I owe everything to my lead dog, Balto!" said Gunnar. The famous musher pointed at the husky sitting patiently nearby. "He's a working dog, like all the others. But he's the best!"

In the daylight, Jack got a good look at Balto. The husky had shaggy black fur, except for white paws and a white chest and a bit of white around his mouth. He had gentle brown eyes.

"You told the mayor that you lost the medicine in an accident at one point," the reporter said.

Gunnar nodded. "Yes, that's right. Yes, I did."

"And how did you find it?" the reporter asked.

"I . . . well, I . . ." The musher shook his head. "I'm not sure. After the accident, I discovered it missing. Somehow the package had come untied from my sled. I panicked and . . . well, I dug around in the snow. And . . . I don't know . . . I guess I just found it."

"It seems like a miracle!" the reporter said.

He turned back to the mayor. "What a disaster it would have been if the medicine were lost on the trail!"

"Indeed," said Mayor Maynard. "The hard work of all the mushers and dogs would have been for nothing. And many more people would have lost their lives to diphtheria. But I have now delivered the package into the hands of Dr. Welch and Nurse Morgan, who will give the lifesaving serum to their patients!"

Everyone clapped and cheered. Oki and his uncle cheered the loudest.

Jack and Annie looked at each other. "Time to go," said Jack.

"Okey dokey," said Annie.

The reporter was asking more questions as Jack and Annie pulled away from the crowd, heading back to the tree house. They hadn't gone far down the boardwalk when they heard barking. They both turned.

"Balto?" said Annie.

The beautiful black husky was bounding after them.

"Balto!" said Annie. She knelt in the blue dawn and reached out her arms.

Balto nearly knocked her over as he licked her face. His dark eyes were twinkling. He seemed to be smiling.

"He remembers us, Jack!" said Annie. "Balto remembers us!"

"Yep," said Jack. "But that's okay. He won't tell anyone."

Annie laughed.

"Balto!" Gunnar Kaasen shouted. "Come!"

The crowd barely glanced at Jack and Annie.

"Balto!" called Gunnar.

"Go on, Balto," Annie said. "You're their hero. They need you."

Balto gave her one more lick. Then he left them and trotted back toward the cheering crowd. His head and tail were held high, his fur fringed with sunlight.

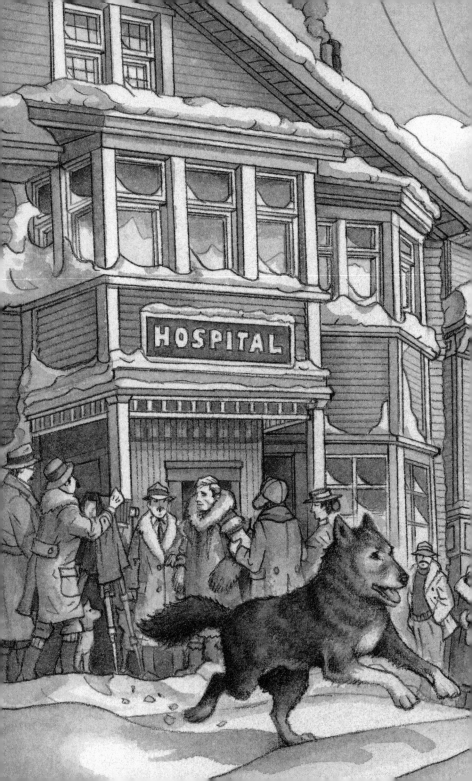

The beautiful black husky was bounding after them.

Jack and Annie turned away and headed down the boardwalk. Soon they left Front Street and walked along the creek. They crossed the bridge and the frosty field to the bare tree with the tree house.

In his thick fur boots and mittens, Jack clumsily climbed the rope ladder. Annie followed him. When they looked out the window, they were nearly blinded by the dazzling reflection of sunlight on the snow and the ice-covered sea.

"Mission accomplished," said Annie.

"I guess we helped save lives," said Jack.

"Yep," said Annie. "Now let's go home and get warm." She picked up the Pennsylvania book and pointed to a picture of the Frog Creek woods.

"I wish we could go there," she said.

The wind started to blow.

The tree house started to spin.

It spun faster and faster.

Then everything was still.

Absolutely still.

CHAPTER TEN

A Gift?

Jack felt warm, wonderfully warm. He was wearing his shorts and T-shirt again. No time at all had passed in Frog Creek. It was still twilight on a summer night.

"Nice," said Annie.

"*Really* nice," said Jack. He reached into his pocket and took out the tiny box, empty of gold dust now. He placed it on the floor of the tree house, next to the guide to the Territory of Alaska.

Annie reached into her pocket and pulled out

the shimmering dark blue box, empty of stardust. She put it beside the gold box on the floor.

"That was a good trip," said Annie.

"Yeah, a little cold, a little stressful," said Jack, "but all in all, very good."

"The best part, of course, was the dogs," said Annie.

"Totally," said Jack. "Come on, let's go. Let's go home." He started down the rope ladder.

"Huskies are great dogs," said Annie, following him.

"Yep," said Jack. "Strong and brave."

"And really smart, too. Like Saint Bernards. Remember Barry in Switzerland?" Annie said as she stepped off the ladder.

"Of course," said Jack. He smiled and shook his head, remembering the giant crazy puppy high in the mountains.

"And remember when Morgan turned Teddy into a terrier?" said Annie.

"Of course," Jack said. "We'd better walk our bikes now. It's getting dark fast."

"Okay," said Annie. She and Jack started pushing their bicycles over leaves and grass.

The woods were filled with the sounds of summer. Bullfrogs croaked from the hidden creek. Crickets chirped in the grass. An owl hooted from a tree branch. Then came another sound: *Yip!*

"What was that?" said Annie, stopping.

"I don't know," said Jack.

Yip!

"It sounds like a dog," said Annie.

"No way," said Jack. "That's too much of a coincidence!"

Yip. Yip!

"Coincidence or not, there's a dog around here somewhere," said Annie. She parked her bike against a tree.

"Seriously?" said Jack.

"Shhh—" said Annie.

The leaves rustled. *Yip. Yip!*

In the dark, Annie got down on her hands and knees. "Where are you?" she whispered.

Yip, yip, yip!

"I've got you!" said Annie, and she lifted a wiggling little black-and-white puppy out of the greenery.

"I don't believe this," said Jack.

"Look—look!" said Annie. She stood up and carried the puppy over to Jack. "Here, pet him."

Jack reached out, and the next thing he knew, his hand was wet from puppy licks. "Oh, man!" he said, laughing.

"Can you push my bike?" Annie asked. "I'll carry him to the street so we can get a good look at him."

Annie took off with the puppy.

Jack tried to steer two bikes through the woods. Annie's bike twisted and fell over, but Jack finally got a good grip and wheeled both bikes out to the sidewalk.

Annie was standing under a streetlamp, cradling the puppy in her arms.

"Let me see him," said Jack. He parked the bikes and looked at the puppy under the light. The tiny dog had beautiful big brown eyes. His curly black-and-white fur was soft and shiny.

"Ohh," said Jack, stroking the furry little head. "He's really cute."

"Let's get him home," said Annie. "I'm sure he's hungry and thirsty."

Jack grabbed their bikes again and started down the sidewalk with Annie and the puppy. "What breed do you think he is?" he asked.

"I think he's a mix," said Annie.

"A mix of *what,* I wonder," said Jack.

"Lots of dogs! All sizes, big, small, and in between. Saint Bernard, terrier, husky," said Annie. "He's a mix of all the dogs we've ever loved."

Jack nodded. "Cool," he said. "I hope Mom and Dad will let us keep him."

"They will," said Annie. "They said we could get a dog when we found the right one. And this is *definitely* the right one."

"Yeah, but what if he's just lost?" said Jack.

"Don't worry. We'll ask around and put up signs," said Annie. "But I have a feeling he's not lost. I think he was actually in the woods waiting for us. I think he's a gift."

The tiny dog had beautiful big brown eyes. His curly black-and-white fur was soft and shiny.

"A gift? From who?" said Jack.

"Maybe from Merlin and Morgan," said Annie. "A gift to thank us."

Jack smiled. He liked that idea. "So what do you think we should name him?" he said.

"Hmm . . ." Annie thought for a moment. "What about Oki?"

"*Oki?*" said Jack. "Like the boy we just met?"

"Yeah, I like that name," said Annie. "Plus, it'll remind us of all the huskies and Balto."

"Yeah . . . ," said Jack. "But, hey, just promise me if he asks to go outside or eat or play with a toy, you won't say 'Okey dokey, Oki.'"

Annie laughed. "I promise," she said.

They climbed the steps to their front porch. Then Annie stopped at the screen door. "Ready to meet the parents?" she asked the puppy.

Yip. Yip!

"Okey dokey, Oki," said Annie. "Let's go inside."

Author's Note

For more than one hundred years, sled dog racing has been a favorite sport in Alaska. The most famous race in sled dog history took place in the winter of 1925, when a relay of sled teams carried a medicine to fight diphtheria from Anchorage, Alaska, up to Nome, Alaska, in less than six days. That wondrous achievement became known as the Great Race of Mercy.

Many brave mushers and their dogs risked their lives in brutal weather to save the diphtheria patients in Nome. The nationwide attention given to their story helped raise awareness about the importance of widespread vaccines to prevent the disease.

Most famous of the dogsled drivers was Leonhard Seppala, who, with the help of his dog Togo, carried the medicine farther than any other driver. Gunnar Kaasen and his lead dog, Balto, received the most accolades from the public because they were the last in the relay and delivered the serum to Nome, where reporters and well-wishers were waiting to celebrate the entire run.

There was some controversy surrounding the fact that Kaasen received so much credit, especially as he had chosen not to stop at the Port Safety roadhouse and allow a musher named Ed Rohn to carry the medicine on the final leg of the trip. Kaasen said that the darkened cabin led him to believe Rohn was sleeping, and therefore time would be wasted by waking him and hitching up all his dogs and getting him on the trail. So Kaasen decided to speed on to Nome to get the medicine there as soon as possible.

Regardless of the debate over who should have received the most credit, the 1925 serum race was testimony to the courage, strength, and skill of *all* the Alaskan mushers and their amazing dog teams.

Today people remember the serum race every spring, when sled drivers and their teams gather to run in the Iditarod, the biggest sporting event of the year in Alaska.

BRING MAGIC TREE HOUSE TO YOUR SCHOOL!

Magic Tree House musicals now available for performance by young people!

Ask your teacher or director
to contact
Music Theatre International
for more information:
BroadwayJr.com
Licensing@MTIshows.com
(212) 541-4684

ATTENTION, TEACHERS!

Classroom Adventures Program

The Magic Tree House **CLASSROOM ADVENTURES PROGRAM** is a free, comprehensive set of online educational resources for teachers developed by Mary Pope Osborne as a gift to teachers, to thank them for their enthusiastic support of the series. Educators can learn more at MTHClassroomAdventures.org.

MAGIC TREE HOUSE